GRANDAD'S BENCH

ADDY FARMER

ILLUSTRATED BY
RUTH RIVERS

**WALKER
BOOKS**

In memory of Grandads P and F
A.F.

In memory of my lovely Dad, John Stewart Rivers 1930-2007
R.R.

First published 2008 by Walker Books Ltd
87 Vauxhall Walk, London SE11 5HJ

2 4 6 8 10 9 7 5 3

Text © 2008 Addy Farmer
Illustrations © 2008 Ruth Rivers

The right of Addy Farmer and Ruth Rivers to be identified as author
and illustrator respectively of this work has been asserted by them in
accordance with the Copyright, Designs and Patents Act 1988

This book has been typeset in Bembo Educational
and Myriad Sketch

Printed and bound in China

British Library Cataloguing in Publication Data:
a catalogue record for this book is available from the British Library

ISBN: 978-1-4063-1139-6

www.walker.co.uk

Autumn
5

Winter
25

Spring
45

Autumn

Jake loved to play in Grandad's
old workshop. He liked the smell of
wood and sawdust. He liked the jumble
of chairs waiting to be repaired
and he liked the neat and tidy
workbench, where all the tools
were lined up, ready to be used.

Best of all he
liked it when Grandad
showed him how to make something.
Jake hopped up onto a stool
next to Grandad.

"Feel this," said Grandad. He gave
Jake a curvy piece of wood as long
and thick as his arm. "I picked it up
from under the scarlet oak."

He pointed out of the little window
above the bench. Jake could see all the
way up to the scarlet oak at the top
of the hill. He stroked the rough bark.
It felt warm. "What will you do with
it?" he asked.

"Watch," said Grandad. He put the wood in a vice and sawed it cleanly in half.

He took one of the halves and planed it flat on both sides. Then he began to chisel.

With delicate little taps he cut out a J. Jake held his breath as an A appeared.

His fingers itched to try it.

"Your turn," said Grandad.

11

Jake's first tap made a big hole. His second tap sliced off the bottom of the A.

"I can't do it like you," he said. He put down the wood and sighed.

Grandad smiled. "I should hope not! It took me years to be this good!" He picked up the chisel. "Come on, you'll be fine. I'll help you."

With Grandad's hand over his, Jake finished off the K and the E.

"Good," said Grandad. "Good enough for an ice-cream before teatime, anyway!"

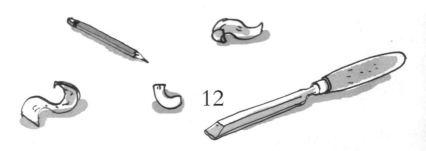

Jake jumped down from the stool
and ran out of the door. It was a late
afternoon in autumn but the sun was
still warm on his face. He charged
through the untidy garden and out
onto the field.

14

"I'll get there first!" he shouted.

"Wait up!" called Grandad. "I'm not so fast today."

"I'll see you up there!" said Jake.

15

Jake ran over the bumpy ground
and all the way up to the scarlet oak.
He lay on his back on a carpet of rich
browns and looked up through the
branches. The leaves glowed red and
orange beneath the setting sun.
The bits of sky between the
leaves fizzed blue-gold.

"It's as old as me, this tree,"
said Grandad, puffing. He leant on
his stick as he fumbled for some coins.
"Tell me the story again," said
Jake, sitting up.

17

"Here, you get the ice-creams first, Jake. You know what I want. I'll stay and watch the skylarks."

Jake darted along the little track
to where the ice-cream van was always
parked. There was a short queue and
Jake looked back. Grandad was gazing
out over the valley. Then he turned
towards Jake. Jake waved and
Grandad waved back.

"Two double cornets with
flakes and sprinkles and raspberry
sauce, please," said Jake.

"Two ice-creams? Are you hungry
today, Jake?" The ice-cream man
smiled.

"No, one's for Grandad," said Jake.
He pointed at the scarlet oak but he
couldn't see Grandad anymore.

The sun dipped further. Jake shivered.
He paid for the ice-creams quickly. He
dropped a penny on the ground but did
not stop to pick it up. He walked fast
towards the scarlet oak. Now he could
see a man kneeling down. He was
speaking into a mobile phone. Jake ran.
The ice-creams streamed long dribbles
onto his hands. He threw them
away. Grandad looked smaller.
He still held his stick even though
he was lying down.

"Grandad!" cried Jake
and he threw himself on
the ground.

Grandad smiled very slowly
and took Jake's hand. His
voice was weak and wobbly.

"Everything will be fine, Jake,"
he whispered.

A cold breeze made the scarlet leaves
rustle, but Jake could still hear the sound
of the ambulance sirens. Someone
put a hand on his shoulder, but Jake
didn't move. He held Grandad's hand
all the way to the hospital. He let go
only when Mum took his hand
and led him away, back home.
Without Grandad.

Winter

Winter was cold and hard
and full of snow. The red and gold
of the autumn leaves had disappeared.
Nothing grew on the scarlet oak.
Its bare branches creaked in the north
wind. The ice-cream van was no
longer parked on the little track.

27

Jake was glad. He never wanted
another ice-cream. No one wanted to
eat ice-cream in the winter anyway.
No one except Grandad, thought Jake.
Grandad liked ice-cream anytime,
anywhere, but best of all, here. Jake
looked up between the branches. The
sky looked down, grey and miserable
and empty. The sun was hidden and
the skylarks were gone.

Jake took off his gloves and touched the bare bark of the trunk. It felt crinkled and warm, like Grandad's hand. But Grandad would never come here again. Not now. Jake wondered how the tree could carry on living now that Grandad had died.

"Hello, Jake!" said Mum "You're
too fast for me!" She put her hands on
her hips and breathed hard. Tiny puffs
of white cloud came out of her mouth.
Her cheeks were as red as the leaves
in autumn. She reached out and took
Jake's hand.

"Did you know that Grandad planted
this tree?" she asked.

Jake nodded and his lip trembled.
He wanted Grandad to tell him
the story again –

about how, when he
was Jake's age, he had carried
an acorn from his garden all the way
up to the top of the hill.

He wanted to hear
how he had planted it in the ground
and watered it every day
for two months.

"He wanted proper shade, so he could watch the skylarks without getting too hot," said Jake.

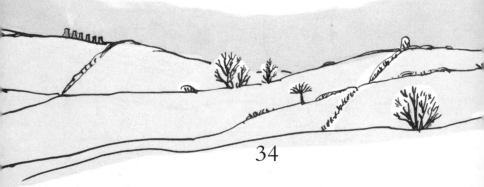

Mum laughed. "That's right. And now the ice-cream van parks here as well! It couldn't be better, could it?"

Jake stared over the valley. He wanted to sit here for ever. It could be better, he thought. If Grandad were here, it *would* be better.

He picked up a fallen branch. It was curvy and rough and as long as his arm. He swung it around, thinking all the time. He wanted to make it better.

"Come on," said Mum.
"I've got a surprise for you."

Back home, Mum led Jake into
Grandad's workshop. He breathed in
the lovely smell of wood and sawdust.
He made his way to the workbench
through the jumble of chairs waiting
to be repaired.

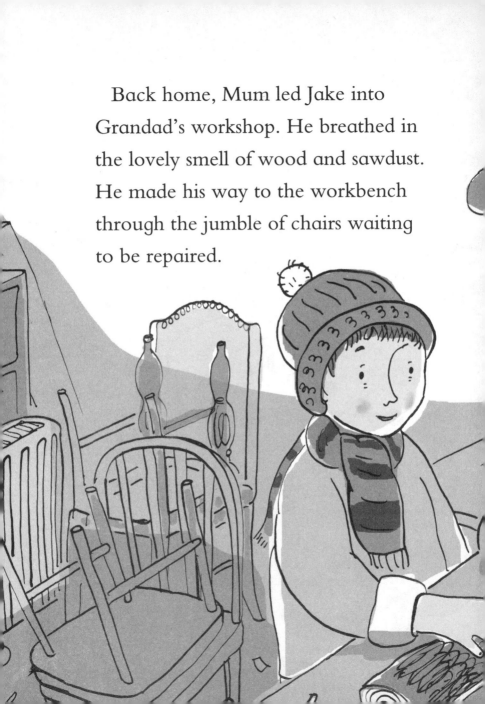

The tools were lined up,
just as Grandad had left them.
Jake put his branch on the bench.
He picked up his nameplate
and stroked the letters.

"The workshop is all yours, Jake,"
said Mum. "Grandad left it to you.
You can do what you want with it."

For a moment Jake could
not see properly. Tears trickled
down his face. The workshop
was full of tools and wood but
there was no Grandad. It all felt empty.

41

"Here," said Mum, and she handed Jake a hanky. She put her arms around him and they looked out of the window. The snow was falling again. "Grandad was a very thoughtful man, Jake."

Through the white, he saw
the dark outline of the scarlet oak.
It waved to him.

"I want to do something for
Grandad, Mum," said Jake. He sniffed.

She looked at him. "You do?"

"Yes," he said, more firmly. "But
I'm going to need your help."

And for the first time since Grandad died, Jake felt happy. He picked up the scarlet oak branch. He knew exactly what he was going to do. Everything was going to be fine.

Spring

45

All through the winter, Jake and Mum worked hard in the workshop. With Mum's help, Jake practised his chiselling on a piece of old wood to get it right. When he could do the letters really well, he took up the scarlet oak branch. He remembered what his grandad had done.

47

Jake told Mum how to put it in a vice and cut it in two with a saw. Then, they planed one half flat on both sides. Finally he took the chisel and began to chip.

Every evening after school they went down to the workshop. Mum sat with her cup of tea. Jake took his time and chiselled. Slowly, slowly the letters appeared, then a whole word, and then it was finished.

By springtime, the wood was smoothed and polished until it shone. It had three coats of varnish, ready for any weather.

It was a sunny, blustery day when everyone met at the scarlet oak. Jake knew them all. His family, his best friends from school and friends of Grandad – they all crowded round Jake's surprise. Even the ice-cream man was there, but not his van. That would be along the little track in time for the school holidays.

Everyone chattered and laughed and even the scarlet oak seemed excited. It rustled and swayed in the wind.

50

When Jake looked up
through its new green leaves, he saw
clouds scudding across a blue sky.
Everything was ready. He looked
at Mum and she began.

"This is all Jake's idea and hard work," she said. "This tree was Dad's favourite place and nobody knows that better than Jake." She turned to him. "Now," she whispered, "it's your turn."

Jake blushed. He didn't want to speak in front of everybody. He coughed. When he spoke his voice was weak and wobbly.

"My grandad planted this tree a long time ago." Behind him was the solid trunk of the scarlet oak. He put his hand on the bark. It felt warm and crinkly, like Grandad's hand. His voice grew stronger. "This was Grandad's tree, his favourite place to watch the skylarks." Jake put both hands on the cloth covering the surprise. "Now anyone can stop here where my grandad stopped. They can watch the skylarks and remember him."

Jake pulled the cover away.

Underneath was a solid wooden
bench that Jake and Mum had bought.
Its corners were rounded and
its iron feet were rooted
in cement.

At the top of the bench was
the most beautiful polished piece
of scarlet oak. Jake had chiselled
out the words clearly and carefully.

GRANDAD'S BENCH

Everyone clapped.

"Sit down on it!" said Mum. "You be the first to sit down on Grandad's bench."

Jake grinned and hopped up onto the seat. It felt brilliant and everyone clapped again.

Lots of people used Grandad's
bench. Jake and Mum came up most
days after school to look at the view.
Sometimes Jake met
his friends
there.

One early
evening, at the start of the school
holidays, he saw that the ice-cream
van was back. He felt sad again as
Mum went to fetch the ice-creams.

He looked over the valley and he listened for the skylarks.

Then he closed his eyes and thought about Grandad. A warm breeze whistled through the scarlet oak.

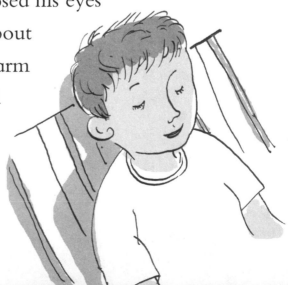

For a moment the tree whispered
to him in Grandad's voice.

"See, we're just fine aren't we, Jake?"

Jake nodded and smiled, and the
breeze moved on.

"Here,
sleepyhead!"
said Mum.
Jake opened
his eyes.

Mum handed him a double cornet
with a flake and sprinkles and
raspberry sauce.

"Here's to Grandad," she said.
She held up the ice-cream.

"And Grandad's bench!" laughed
Jake, and he took an enormous
bite of his ice-cream.

It was sweet
and creamy and
delicious.